KT-561-957

THIS BOOK

BELONGS TO:

klara

....

....

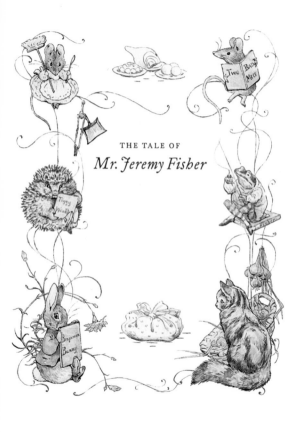

THE TALE OF
Mr. Jeremy Fisher

THE TALE OF
MR. JEREMY FISHER

BY

BEATRIX POTTER

A PETER RABBIT™

110th Anniversary Edition

FREDERICK WARNE

FOR STEPHANIE
FROM COUSIN B.

FREDERICK WARNE

Published by the Penguin Group
Penguin Books Ltd., 80 Strand, London WC2R 0RL, England
Penguin Group (USA) Inc., 375 Hudson Street, New York, New York 10014, USA
Penguin Group (Australia), 250 Camberwell Road, Camberwell,
Victoria 3124, Australia (a division of Pearson Australia Group Pty. Ltd.)
Penguin Group (Canada), 90 Eglinton Avenue East, Suite 700, Toronto,
Ontario M4P 2Y3, Canada (a division of Pearson Penguin Canada Inc.)
Penguin Books India Pvt. Ltd., 11 Community Centre, Panchsheel Park, New Delhi—110 017, India
Penguin Group (NZ), 67 Apollo Drive, Rosedale, Auckland 0632,
New Zealand (a division of Pearson New Zealand Ltd.)
Penguin Books (South Africa) (Pty.) Ltd., 24 Sturdee Avenue, Rosebank, Johannesburg 2196, South Africa

Penguin Books Ltd., Registered Offices: 80 Strand, London WC2R 0RL, England

Website: www.peterrabbit.com

First published by Frederick Warne in 1906
First published with reset text and new reproductions
of Beatrix Potter's illustrations in 2002
This edition published in 2011

003 - 10 9 8 7 6 5 4 3

New reproductions copyright © Frederick Warne & Co., 2002
Original copyright in text and illustrations © Frederick Warne & Co., 1906
Frederick Warne & Co. is the owner of all rights, copyrights and trademarks
in the Beatrix Potter character names and illustrations.

All rights reserved. Without limiting the rights under copyright reserved
above, no part of this publication may be reproduced, stored in or introduced
into a retrieval system, or transmitted in any form or by any means
(electronic, mechanical, photocopying, recording or otherwise), without
the prior written permission of the above publisher of this book.

Colour reproduction by
EAE Creative Colour Ltd, Norwich
Printed and bound in China

PUBLISHER'S NOTE

Mr. Jeremy Fisher was first introduced in September 1893, in a picture letter to Noel Moore, the youngest son of Beatrix's last governess. However, *The Tale of Mr. Jeremy Fisher* was not published until 1906.

Like other publishers who she had previously sent her work to, Frederick Warne & Co. had reservations about the main character being a frog. It was thought that frogs were generally less appealing than fluffier characters. Beatrix, however, convinced her editor that the flower backgrounds could be an attractive enough project and *The Tale of Mr. Jeremy Fisher* is one of her prettiest and most popular books.

ONCE UPON A TIME there was a frog called Mr. Jeremy Fisher; he lived in a little damp house amongst the buttercups at the edge of a pond.

THE water was all slippy-sloppy in the larder and in the back passage.

But Mr. Jeremy liked getting his feet wet; nobody ever scolded him, and he never caught a cold!

9

HE was quite pleased when he looked out and saw large drops of rain, splashing in the pond—

"I WILL get some worms and go fishing and catch a dish of minnows for my dinner," said Mr. Jeremy Fisher. "If I catch more than five fish, I will invite my friends Mr. Alderman Ptolemy Tortoise and Sir Isaac Newton. The Alderman, however, eats salad."

MR. JEREMY put on a macintosh, and a pair of shiny goloshes; he took his rod and basket, and set off with enormous hops to the place where he kept his boat.

THE boat was round and green, and very like the other lily-leaves. It was tied to a water-plant in the middle of the pond.

MR. JEREMY took a reed pole, and pushed the boat out into open water. "I know a good place for minnows," said Mr. Jeremy Fisher.

MR. JEREMY stuck his pole into the mud and fastened the boat to it.

Then he settled himself cross-legged and arranged his fishing tackle. He had the dearest little red float. His rod was a tough stalk of grass, his line was a fine long white horse-hair, and he tied a little wriggling worm at the end.

THE rain trickled down his back, and for nearly an hour he stared at the float.

"This is getting tiresome, I think I should like some lunch," said Mr. Jeremy Fisher.

He punted back again amongst the water-plants, and took some lunch out of his basket.

"I will eat a butterfly sandwich, and wait till the shower is over," said Mr. Jeremy Fisher.

A GREAT big water-beetle came up underneath the lily leaf and tweaked the toe of one of his goloshes.

Mr. Jeremy crossed his legs up shorter, out of reach, and went on eating his sandwich.

ONCE or twice something moved about with a rustle and a splash amongst the rushes at the side of the pond.

"I trust that is not a rat," said Mr. Jeremy Fisher; "I think I had better get away from here."

MR. JEREMY shoved the boat out again a little way, and dropped in the bait. There was a bite almost directly; the float gave a tremendous bobbit!

"A minnow! a minnow! I have him by the nose!" cried Mr. Jeremy Fisher, jerking up his rod.

BUT what a horrible surprise! Instead of a smooth fat minnow, Mr. Jeremy landed little Jack Sharp the stickleback, covered with spines!

THE stickleback floundered about the boat, pricking and snapping until he was quite out of breath. Then he jumped back into the water.

AND a shoal of other little fishes
put their heads out, and laughed
at Mr. Jeremy Fisher.

AND while Mr. Jeremy sat disconsolately on the edge of his boat — sucking his sore fingers and peering down into the water — a *much* worse thing happened; a really *frightful* thing it would have been, if Mr. Jeremy had not been wearing a macintosh!

A GREAT big enormous trout came up — ker-pflop-p-p-p! with a splash — and it seized Mr. Jeremy with a snap, "Ow! Ow! Ow!" — and then it turned and dived down to the bottom of the pond!

BUT the trout was so displeased with the taste of the macintosh, that in less than half a minute it spat him out again; and the only thing it swallowed was Mr. Jeremy's goloshes.

MR. JEREMY bounced up to the surface of the water, like a cork and the bubbles out of a soda water bottle; and he swam with all his might to the edge of the pond.

HE scrambled out on the first bank he came to, and he hopped home across the meadow with his macintosh all in tatters.

"WHAT a mercy that was not a pike!" said Mr. Jeremy Fisher. "I have lost my rod and basket; but it does not much matter, for I am sure I should never have dared to go fishing again!"

HE put some sticking plaster on his fingers, and his friends both came to dinner. He could not offer them fish, but he had something else in his larder.

SIR ISAAC NEWTON wore his
black and gold waistcoat,

AND Mr. Alderman Ptolemy Tortoise brought a salad with him in a string bag.

AND instead of a nice dish of minnows — they had a roasted grasshopper with ladybird sauce; which frogs consider a beautiful treat; but *I* think it must have been nasty!

THE END